You walk through the door of Jake's Place. The smells of a hundred different foods dance in the air. Your stomach starts quietly growling. You start thinking about what you want for lunch. All of a sudden, Fred's voice snaps you out of your food trance.

"Hey, back here!" Fred calls. You see Fred waving at you to join the gang at their table. You walk to the back of the restaurant. Fred, Daphne, Velma, Shaggy, and Scooby are sitting around a big table. They have menus in front of them.

Daphne smiles. "Thanks for coming," she says. "I hope you're hungry."

"This restaurant is famous for its extremely large portions," Velma explains. "And something else a little unusual."

"Like what?" you ask.

You hear a cart with a squeaky wheel burst through the kitchen doors.

"Who wants a roll?" shouts the man pushing the cart. "Hot rolls, comin' at ya! Who wants a roll?"

People all over the restaurant raise their hands. The man starts tossing hot rolls to the customers.

"Like, I could use a little before-lunch snack," Shaggy says. "How about you, Scooby-Doo?"

"Rou bet!" Scooby says. He raises a paw into the air. Shaggy raises his hand. Scooby raises another paw. Shaggy raises his other hand. Scooby then raises his tail.

"No fair, Scoob," complains Shaggy.

The man behind the cart sees Shaggy and Scooby and tosses five rolls in their direction. Shaggy and Scooby catch the

SCOOBY-DOO! and YOU:
THE CASE OF THE WANDERING WITCH

A Collect the Clues Mystery

By James Gelsey

WORLDWIDE PUBLISHING™

SCHOLASTIC INC.
New York   Toronto   London   Auckland   Sydney
Mexico City   New Delhi   Hong Kong

ISBN 0-439-23151-5

12 11 10 9 8 7 6 5 4 3 2   0 1 2 3 4 5/0

Cover and interior illustrations by Duendes del Sur
Cover and interior design by Madalina Stefan

Printed in the U.S.A.

First Scholastic printing, December 2000

rolls and then quickly drop them on the table.

"What's the matter, Shaggy?" Daphne asks. "Can't handle a few little dinner rolls?"

"Man, these things aren't rolls," Shaggy says. "They're more like fire balls. Right, Scoob?"

Scooby is too busy gobbling up his three rolls to pay attention to Shaggy.

"The way you dropped those rolls, Shaggy, reminds me of something else you dropped," Velma says.

"What do you mean, Velma?" Shaggy asks.

"She means the magic witch's ball you dropped during our last mystery," Fred adds.

"Like, why'd you have to bring that up, man?" Shaggy says. "Just thinking about it gives me the creeps."

"It *was* kind of a creepy mystery," Daphne agrees. "And a pretty tough one to solve, too."

"I'll bet you would have been able to solve it without any problem," says Velma.

"If you want, we'll show you our Clue Keeper," Fred offers. "That way you can take a crack at it yourself. What do you say?"

"You bet!" you exclaim without even thinking.

Daphne reaches into her pocketbook and takes out a small notebook. She hands it to you.

"It was my turn to put everything that happened in the Clue Keeper," Daphne explains. "And I took some pretty good notes. Everything you need to know is in there.

Remember, when you see  you've just met a suspect."

"And a  tells you that you've just found a clue," continues Fred. "After each entry, we'll ask you some questions to help you along."

"So keep your own Clue Keeper and a pencil handy," Velma says. "And good luck solving *The Case of the Wandering Witch*."

Clue Keeper Entry 1

"Well, here we are, gang," Fred said as he parked the van. "Galaxy Pictures, home of *The Wandering Witch.*"

Scooby's ears perked up.

"Huh?" he said.

"Like, did you say *witch*?" Shaggy asked. "As in black pointy hat and broomstick?"

"I guess so," Fred replied.

"Then Scoob and I will get out here," Shaggy said. "Because the only kind of witch we want to be around is the kind you make with two pieces of bread."

"What kind of a witch is that?" Velma asked.

"A sandwich," Shaggy answered. "Get it? A sandwich?" He and Scooby laughed.

"Very funny, you two," I said. "But *The Wandering Witch* isn't a real witch. It's the name of the movie we're going to see."

"Why didn't you say so?" said Shaggy. "Scoob and I love the movies. So let's quit talking and start walking. C'mon, Scoob old pal."

Shaggy and Scooby jumped out of the van. Fred, Velma, and I followed.

"Boy, we're lucky your uncle could get us these tickets, Daph," Fred said.

"I know," I replied.

We walked across the parking lot to Building A. A woman holding a large picket sign walked around in front of the building.

"'A cow says wander by *The Wandering Witch*,'" Velma read.

Shaggy laughed when he heard this.

"What's so funny?" asked the woman holding the sign.

"Like, I didn't know that cows could talk," Shaggy said.

The woman frowned at Shaggy.

"The sign doesn't say 'a cow,'" the woman explained. "It says ACOW. It stands for the American Council of Witches. I'm Jayne Torrance, the president." 👁 👁

"Why are you picketing out here?" I asked.

"ACOW is planning a boycott of the movie," Jayne replied.

Shaggy and Scooby couldn't help but giggle. I gave them a sharp look to remind them to behave.

Jayne continued, "The members of my organization are extremely angry about the way that witches are portrayed."

"So you're the one sending me all those e-mails," said a man who had quietly joined us. "It's nice to finally meet you in person."

Jayne looked puzzled.

"I'm Bucky Lowell, the director," the man said. "And you must be Jayne Torrance from that witches group. Thanks for coming to the sneak preview. Now maybe you'll see you've got nothing to complain about."

"I hope you're right," Jayne replied. "Because, believe me, you don't want to get ACOW angry."

"'Cause, man, there's nothing worse than an angry cow," Shaggy whispered to Scooby. The two of them started to giggle.

Bucky Lowell turned and looked at us.

"And you are . . . ?" he asked.

I stepped forward. "I'm Daphne Blake," I said. "And these are my friends. This is Fred, Velma, Shaggy, and Scooby-Doo."

"Glad you could join us today," Bucky said. "I'll tell ya, this is going to be one un-

forgettable afternoon. Why don't you go inside and have some refreshments before we
get started?"

"Refreshments?" Shaggy asked. "Now
you're talking. Last one inside is a stale bag
of popcorn!" He and Scooby raced to the
door.

Fred, Velma, and I said good-bye to
Jayne.

"It was nice meeting you, Jayne," Fred said. "I guess we'll see you inside."

"Are you kidding?" Jayne replied. "I wouldn't miss it for the world. It's not every day you get invited to a studio sneak preview at a big movie studio. I'll be in just before the movie starts."

"Hey, Fred, hurry up, man," Shaggy called. "Like, we need the tickets to get inside. Scooby and I are starving!"

"I don't know what they like more," I whispered to Fred and Velma. "The movie or the popcorn." The three of us laughed as we walked to the door.

Shaggy's Mystery-Solving Tips

"Like, did you catch the 👁 👁 in this entry? Man, they sure give me the creeps every time I see them. But they also tip you off to a suspect. Get your Clue Keeper and answer these questions."

1. What is the suspect's name?

2. What does she do?

3. Why is she at Galaxy Pictures on that afternoon?

"Now grab yourself a hot roll (if you can) and get ready for the next Clue Keeper entry."

Clue Keeper Entry 2

We walked through the doors and into Building A. "Zoinks!" Shaggy exclaimed. "That is one scary-looking witch." He pointed to a mannequin dressed like a witch that was just inside the doors of the screening room.

We walked back to the lobby. It looked like a regular movie theater. The walls were lined with big posters for other movies. And off to one side there was an enormous stand.

"Man, oh, man," gasped Shaggy. "Like, you three enjoy the movie. Scoob and I will meet you afterwards over there." Shaggy started walking over to the food concession stand.

"Hold on, Shaggy," Fred said. "We're all going to see the movie together."

"Don't bother," a strange voice behind us said. We all turned and saw a woman dressed in gray and black.

"You're Bonnie LaRue!" Velma exclaimed. "The famous screenwriter!"

"Famous? I don't know about that," the woman answered. "I am a screenwriter, but between you and me, I don't want any credit for this film."

"Now, now, Bonnie," Bucky Lowell said as he walked by. "Don't despair. The film's terrific!"

"There's nothing terrific about it," Bonnie said angrily. "You took my script and ruined it by changing almost every line. See?" Bonnie held up a thick script and waved it at Bucky.

"The new lines I wrote us aren't changes," Bucky said. "They're improvements."

"Just take my name off the credits," Bonnie replied. "The movie you made is not the same movie I wrote." She threw her script on the ground.

"But you're the hottest screenwriter in town," Bucky complained. "If we take your name off, people may not want to come to see the film."

"That will be fine by me," she said. Bonnie turned and walked away angrily. Fred bent down and picked up the script.

"Bucky, why are there so many colored pages in this script?" he asked.

"Every time we make changes in the script, we print the changes on colored paper so everyone knows which lines are new," Bucky explained. "I hope you kids enjoy the film. See you inside the theater." Bucky continued on his way.

"Jinkies," Velma said, flipping through the script. "It looks to me like there are more colored pages than plain ones."

"I guess that explains why Bonnie is so mad," I suggested.

"Like, I don't know about the rest of you, but I'm starving," Shaggy said.

"*Re, roo,*" Scooby agreed.

"Then let's go get that popcorn, Scoob," Shaggy said.

Fred's Mystery-Solving Tips

"**D**id you notice the 👀 in Entry 2? Grab your pen or pencil and your Clue Keeper and answer these questions."

1. What is the suspect's name?

2. What is her connection to the movie?

3. What is she angry about that could make her a suspect?

"Ready for more? Then read on!"

Clue Keeper Entry 3

The three of us walked over to the concession stand and stood behind Shaggy and Scooby. They were standing in front of the counter looking at all of the goodies.

"Have you made up your mind yet?" asked the woman standing behind the counter. She was dressed in a red usher's uniform.

Shaggy looked at the woman behind the counter. "We'll have one humongous popcorn, please." The woman started filling a truly humongous bucket with popcorn. Suddenly, the lights flashed in the lobby.

"Man, looks like someone forget to pay the electric bill," Shaggy said.

"That just means the movie's about to begin," the woman said. "And you don't want to miss the beginning. If you do, you'll be lost for the rest of the movie."

"How do you know about the movie?" I asked. "I thought no one's seen it yet."

"I'm in it," the woman replied.

"You're an actress?" I asked.

"My name is Lydia Monroe," the woman replied.

Shaggy took the humongous bucket of popcorn and asked, "If you're an actress, like, what are you doing selling popcorn?"

"Shaggy!" I scolded.

"That's all right," the woman said. "I really should have said I *was* in the movie. I'm working here so I can pay my bills. My part was the first thing Bucky cut. He felt my character didn't fit into the story."

"I'm sorry to hear that," Fred said.

"Thanks," she said. "But I really hope the only person who's going to be sorry is Bucky Lowell. I gave up a major role in another

movie to be in this one. But when Bucky cut my part, it was too late for me to get anything else. I hope this movie ruins Bucky's career the way he ruined mine."

The lights flashed again.

"You'd better hurry inside," Lydia said. "This may be your only chance to ever see the movie." She put a CLOSED sign on top of the counter and walked to the far end of the concession stand.

"Let's go," Fred said. We hurried out of the lobby and into the movie theater.

There couldn't have been more than ten rows of seats, and almost every single one was full. A narrow aisle divided the theater in half. Up at the front, a big red curtain hung in front of the movie screen. We couldn't find five seats together, but Velma found two seats up front and three off to the side in the back.

"Like, Scooby and I will sit up front," Shaggy said. "Best seats in the house. Come on, Scoob. Let's open the lunch we brought from home. Sandwiches go great with popcorn."

"Just be careful, you two," Velma called. "And don't cause any trouble."

"Like, we're in a movie theater, Velma," Shaggy said. "What trouble could we possibly cause?"

"We don't want to find out," I replied with a smile.

21

"I hope you noticed the 👁 👁 in Entry 3. They tipped you off about our third suspect. Get your pen or pencil and open up your Clue Keeper. I've got some questions to help you organize your notes."

1. What is the suspect's name?

2. What is she doing in the movie theater?

3. What happened to her that could make her a possible suspect?

"Now that you've met your final suspect, you're ready to see what happened during the sneak preview of *The Wandering Witch*."

22

Clue Keeper Entry 4

Shaggy and Scooby walked down the aisle to the front of the theater. Fred, Velma, and I sat down in three empty seats in back of them. Bucky Lowell stood on the small stage in front of the screen. Everyone stopped talking and looked up at Bucky. The only sound in the whole movie theater came from up front. It was the sound of munching. Shaggy and Scooby looked up and saw Bucky looking at them.

"Like, sorry, man," Shaggy said.

Shaggy stopped eating his sandwich and put the popcorn bucket on the floor. Bucky looked back at the audience.

"Thank you for coming this afternoon,"
Bucky began. Sit back, relax, and enjoy this
special sneak preview of *The Wandering
Witch.*"

Everyone applauded as Bucky returned
to his seat. The lights in the theater dimmed
as the big red curtain slowly parted, reveal-
ing the movie screen.

Just as the movie started, a big puff of
smoke filled the center aisle. When it

cleared, we all saw someone standing in front of the movie screen. It was a witch!

Angrily, Bucky walked down the aisle.

"Come no further!" the witch warned. "Or I'll light you up like this movie screen."

"Ha!" Bucky replied. "I dare you!"

"Let this be a lesson to all of you!" the witch screamed. She reached into her sleeve and threw something right at Bucky.

It exploded into a puff of smoke. When the

smoke cleared, everyone gasped. "Zoinks!" Shaggy shouted. "Like, his face is glowing!"

It was true. Bucky Lowell's face and body seemed to be glowing in the dark.

"Heed my warning," the witch hissed at the rest of us. "And leave while you still have the chance!" The witch's cackle filled the theater. Smoke filled the stage again. When the smoke had cleared, the witch was gone. And so was Bucky Lowell.

"Quick, let's get out of here, Scoob!" Shaggy cried. He and Scooby jumped up from their seats. Everyone else in the theater also jumped up and ran toward the door.

"It looks like we've got a real mystery on our hands," Fred said to Velma and me. "Time to get to work."

Clue Keeper Entry 5

Before we could look for clues, the first thing we had to do was find Shaggy and Scooby.

"I'll bet I know where they're hiding," Velma said. "Why don't you two look around for clues in here? I'll go out into the lobby, get Shaggy and Scooby, and see if I find anything out there."

"Sounds like a plan," Fred said.

Velma went back into the lobby. She didn't see Scooby and Shaggy so she headed outside to look.

Velma walked away as Shaggy and

27

Scooby climbed out of the cabinet. (They told me all this later.)

"Let's look around Scoob," Shaggy said. "You start at that end, and I'll start at this end." Scooby walked to the far end of the concession stand. He put his nose to the ground and slowly started sniffing around for clues. Shaggy walked to the other end and got down on his hands and knees. He looked all over for clues. When Shaggy and Scooby met back in the middle, they stood up.

"Rikes!" Scooby shouted.

"Zoinks!" exclaimed Shaggy.

The witch was standing on the other side of the counter.

"Do you have any witch's treats?" she asked with a cackle.

Scooby jumped into Shaggy's arms. Shaggy ran down to the far end of the concession stand, but there was no way out.

"Man, oh man!" Shaggy exclaimed. They ran back to the other end of the concession stand, but the witch was standing there. As they ran back, Shaggy and Scooby jumped back into the cabinet and closed the door. A few moments later, Velma opened the cabinet.

"Enough clowning around, you two," Velma scolded. "We'll never solve this mystery if you keep acting like this."

"But that witch showed up again," Shaggy said. "She chased us around the concession stand."

"Then where is she?" Velma asked, looking around.

"We don't know," Shaggy replied. "But maybe we'd better go find Fred and Daphne before she comes back."

"Since we didn't find any clues, we may as well," Velma said.

Velma turned and walked back to the movie theater doors. Shaggy and Scooby climbed out of the closet again. As they walked out of the concession stand, Shaggy noticed something on the floor.

"Hey, Velma!" Shaggy called. "You dropped something." He picked it up and ran over to Velma.

"This is a ticket to get into the movie theater for the sneak preview," Velma said. "I'll bet the witch dropped it when she was chasing you. Let's show it to Fred and Daphne." Velma walked back into the movie theater.

Shaggy and Scooby stopped to look at another big witch mannequin standing in the lobby.

"You know, Scoob," Shaggy said. "She's

not really so scary."

Suddenly, Shaggy and Scooby heard the witch's cackle.

"Zoinks! Let's get outta here!" Shaggy exclaimed.

Shaggy and Scooby zoomed out of the lobby and back into the movie theater.

Velma's Mystery-Solving Tips

"It looks like Shaggy and Scooby found an interesting clue. Did you find it, too? Great. Now open up your Clue Keeper and answer these questions about it. You'll be well on your way to solving this mystery."

1. What clue did you find in this entry?

2. What do you think the clue has to do with the witch?

3. Which of the suspects could have dropped this clue?

Clue Keeper Entry 6

Shaggy and Scooby burst through the movie theater doors.

"Make way!" Shaggy shouted. "There's a witch after us!" He and Scooby ran down the aisle and jumped onto the stage. In the blink of an eye, they were hiding behind the heavy red curtain.

"All right, you two," I said. "Come on out. There's no witch in here."

It became very quiet onstage. We couldn't even hear Scooby's knees knocking together like they do when he is really scared.

"Something's up," Fred said. "Come on."

We all climbed up onto the stage. Fred pulled back the curtain.

"Jinkies! They're gone!" Velma exclaimed.

And it was true. Instead of Shaggy and Scooby, all we could see was the wall. Velma took a closer look.

"Do you see what I see?" she asked.

Fred and I also got closer. We could barely make out the outline of a large rectangle on the wall.

"We do now," Fred answered. He ran his hand along the outline. At one place, he pushed against the door. We all heard a "click" and the rectangle moved. It was a door!

The door opened into a small utility closet. And inside, Shaggy was standing on a small crate, holding Scooby in his arms.

"Like, don't you guys know how to knock?" Shaggy asked.

"Enough fooling around," Velma said. "Come on out so we can look for more clues."

"But what about the witch?" Shaggy asked.

34

"There's no witch here," I answered. "It's perfectly safe."

Scooby jumped out of Shaggy's arms. Shaggy started to step off the crate, but he lost his balance. He tumbled to the floor, knocking the crate over. Underneath it was another crate which was a little smaller than the first. The words *Property of Galaxy Pictures* were stamped in big white letters across the side. Fred opened the top.

Inside we found all kinds of makeup, from lipsticks to eye shadows to foundations to fake eyebrows to colored contact lenses. We also found a bag of small white balls.

"Hey, look, Scooby," Shaggy said. "Ping-Pong balls. Let's have a catch."

Shaggy grabbed one of the white balls. He tossed it gently to Scooby. Scooby caught the ball. Scooby then pretended to be a baseball pitcher. He stood straight up and held the ball in his front paws. He pretended to look over to first base. Then he pretended to get a signal from the catcher. Scooby went into his wind-up and threw the ball to Shaggy.

Scooby threw the ball so hard, when Shaggy caught it, the ball exploded into a puff of smoke.

After the smoke cleared, the strangest thing happened.

"Shaggy," I said. "You're glowing!"

"Jinkies!" Velma exclaimed. "You look just like Bucky Lowell did."

Shaggy looked down at his arms.

"Zoinks!" he exclaimed. "That witch has turned me into a human lightbulb!"

"The witch had nothing to do with it, Shaggy," Velma said. "It's only makeup. See?" She walked over and wiped her finger on Shaggy's arm. Her fingertip also glowed.

"This clue certainly sheds new light on the mystery," Velma said.

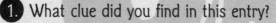

Daphne's Mystery-Solving Tips

"**W**e found a pretty amazing clue in that closet. Did you find it, too? Great. Now get out your Clue Keeper and answer these questions."

1. What clue did you find in this entry?

2. Which of the suspects do you think would be able to get their hands on it?

3. Who do you think would know how to use it?

"You're doing a great job so far. Keep it up!"

Clue Keeper Entry 7

"Shaggy, you should get yourself cleaned up," I suggested. "Why don't you go to the restroom in the lobby?"

"That's all right, Daph, I'll just use this," Shaggy said. He took a black scarf out of his pocket and started wiping his face with it.

"Where did you get that?" asked Velma.

"Like, I found it behind the concession stand," Shaggy said. "I wanted to have it just in case Scooby and I needed to wave a sur-render flag."

"But you don't use a black flag to surren-der," I said. "You use a white flag."

"I know that, but I couldn't find anything white in the bag," Shaggy continued.

Fred, Daphne, and I looked at one another.

"What bag, Shaggy?" Fred asked.

"The one in the cabinet behind the concession stand," Shaggy answered. "Like, weren't you listening?"

The five of us climbed down off the stage and went back into the lobby. We headed straight for the concession stand. Velma led us to the cabinet where she had found Shaggy and Scooby hiding. She opened the cabinet door. A big shopping bag was tucked far in the back. Fred dumped it on the floor. Three things fell out: a pair of shoes, one of those white balls we found in the makeup kit, and a script. Fred picked up the script and looked at the cover.

"It's a script for the movie," Fred said. "It sure looks different from Bonnie's script. It seems really thin."

"Hmmm, things are starting to fall into place," Fred said. "Gang, it's time to set a trap."

"What kind of trap?" someone asked.

We all turned around and saw Bucky Lowell standing there.

"Mr. Lowell!" I exclaimed. "What are you doing here?"

"And, like, why aren't you glowing anymore?" Shaggy asked.

Bucky laughed.

"I didn't fall for that smoke screen stuff or glow-in-the-dark makeup trick like everyone else," Bucky explained. "I knew that the witch up there wasn't a real witch. So I decided to have some fun and rewrite that witch's script and make myself disappear, too."

"How'd you do it?" Fred asked. "We couldn't find any doors except the ones to the lobby and that closet next to the movie screen."

"Nothing to it, really," Bucky said. "Since everyone was looking at the stage, I was able to sneak out the doors to the lobby. From there I went to my office."

"So you wanted everyone to think that

the witch made you disappear," Velma asked.

"Right. That way I could buy myself some time trying to figure out who's behind all this," Bucky said. "But it looks like you beat me to it."

"In that case, we sure could use your help in catching the witch," Fred said. "What do you say?"

"I say that for this scene, you kids can call the shots," replied Bucky.

"So, you found the clue in this entry, right? It's pretty cool. If you can answer these questions in your own Clue Keeper, you'll agree that this last clue really helps things fall into place. Good luck."

1. What clue did you find in this entry?

2. What does this clue have to with the movie?

3. Who is most likely connected to this clue?

Clue Keeper Entry 8

"Okay everyone, here's my plan," Fred said. "The witch will come back if she thinks the screening is going to continue. So, Bucky, you're going to be the bait and wait inside the movie theater. Shaggy and I will hide on the stage ready to wrap her in the curtain. Daphne, you and Velma will run the movie projector from the booth."

"Like, what about Scooby-Doo?" Shaggy asked.

"Scooby has the most important job," Fred continued. "Scooby, you're going to distract the witch long enough for Shaggy and I to catch her."

"Ruh-uh," Scooby said. *"Rot ree."*

"Please, Scooby," I begged.

"Will you do it for a Scooby Snack?" Velma asked.

Scooby's left ear perked up a bit, but the rest of him didn't move.

"All right, how about two?" Velma said.

"Rokay!" Scooby said happily. His tail wagged and his big pink tongue licked his lips.

Velma and I each tossed a Scooby Snack into the air. Scooby gobbled them down together.

"Finally," Fred said. "Bucky, I'll need your help with the curtain."

"And we'll take care of Scooby," I offered. I walked over to the mannequin and grabbed the witch's hat and black robe. Velma and I dressed Scooby in them.

"Like, Scooby-Doo, you make a pretty good witch," Shaggy said.

"There's only one thing missing," Velma said.

46

"What's that?" Shaggy asked.

"You!" she replied. "For this to work, you're going to have to be Scooby's voice."

"You can stand behind the curtain on the stage," I said.

"Man, I knew I should have kept my big mouth shut," Shaggy moaned.

Fred and Bucky came out of the movie theater.

"Everything ready, Fred?" Velma asked.

"All set," Fred said. "Scooby, try to get the witch to come onto the stage. We rigged the curtain so Shaggy and I will be able to yank it down and use it as a net."

"Since I have to be in the theater, I want to show you how to run the projector," Bucky said. "Let's go."

Fred, Shaggy, and Scooby went into the movie theater. Velma and I followed Bucky to the projection booth. When we got inside, Bucky showed us how to turn the projector on and off.

"When the witch shows up, dial 617 on the phone over there for studio security," Bucky said. "You can start the projector when you see me sit down."

Bucky left the projection booth. We looked through the small projection window and saw him walk into the theater and sit down. Velma turned on the projector. The lights in the theater automatically dimmed.

The movie had only run for a couple of minutes when a puff of smoke filled the aisle. When it cleared, the witch was standing at the front of the theater.

"I warned you, Bucky Lowell!" she shouted. "Now you and this film will be cursed for all time!"

Just as she raised her arms to cast her spell, Scooby jumped out from behind the curtain.

"Like, how dare you come here and impersonate a witch!" Shaggy said through the curtain. He disguised his voice a bit and made it sound higher and meaner. "I am the only real witch here!"

The witch stopped what she was doing and stared at Scooby.

"No, I am the only real witch!" the witch said angrily, jumping onto the stage. "Now get out of here before I light you up like this movie screen." The witch reached into her robe.

"Now, Fred!" Velma and I yelled from the projection booth.

Startled, the witch looked up at us. Fred yanked the rope. But instead of Fred and Shaggy catching the curtain, the curtain caught them.

"Ruh-oh!" Scooby said. He reached into his robe and took out one of the white makeup balls. The witch held one in her hand, too. Shaggy managed to get free of the curtain and stood up.

"Zoinks!" he shouted when he saw the witch.

The witch looked over at the curtain and threw her ball at Shaggy.

"Man, not again!" Shaggy moaned.

Scooby threw his ball at the witch and then jumped off the stage. I took the headband out of my hair and covered the lens of the projector. The theater went dark except for two moving lights: Shaggy and the witch, who were both glowing in the dark.

"She's hiding in the fifth row!" Velma called.

Fred and Bucky caught up to her and made sure she couldn't get away. Velma turned off the projector. The lights in the theater slowly came back on. We ran downstairs and back into the theater.

"Now let's see who's really behind all this," Fred said.

You close the Clue Keeper and look up at the gang.

"Well, you've met all the suspects and found all the clues," Fred says. "Do you think you're up to solving the mystery?"

You nod your head.

"Great," Daphne says. "Here's some advice. Look at your list of suspects and clues and answer these questions."

"First, who do you think had a good rea-

53

son to want to get back at Bucky Lowell and scare people away from the movie?" Velma asks.

"Second, who do you think would be able to get the things they needed from around the movie studio?" Fred asks.

"Third, who do you think was the most careless in leaving us a very important clue?" Daphne asks.

"See if you can eliminate any of the suspects first," Velma suggests. "Then, using all of the information you've collected, as well as your own smarts, try to figure out who's pretending to be the witch."

It looks like Shaggy's going to want to stay until he manages to catch and eat one of those hot rolls. Take your time, and when you're done, turn the page and we'll tell you what really happened.

"**T**he witch was really Lydia Monroe," Daphne says. "I'll bet you figured that out, didn't you?"

Before you can nod your head, Velma continues.

"But I'll bet it wasn't easy," she says. "Even we had a hard time at first because all of the suspects had such good reasons for wanting to ruin the sneak preview."

"But once we started piecing the clues together," Fred explains, "we were able to start eliminating suspects."

"The first clue we found was the pass to get into the screening, remember?" Daphne says. "A real witch would never need a pass to get into anywhere. But since security was so tight, all three of the suspects did need a pass."

"While that clue didn't rule anyone out," Fred continues, "the next one did. Only someone with access to other parts of the studio would be able to get their hands on a whole makeup kit."

"Which ruled out Jayne Torrance," Daphne says. "You remember her, right? The president of ACOW?"

"That left Bonnie LaRue and Lydia Monroe," Velma says. "Both of them spent a lot of time at the studio and could have easily gotten the makeup kit."

"But the last clue was the most important one," Fred says.

"The script was really skinny," Daphne says. "I remember making careful note of that in the Clue Keeper. Did you notice that? It wasn't full of colored pages like Bonnie LaRue's script."

"Which means it belonged to someone who wasn't around to get all of Bucky's rewrites," Velma said. "Someone whose part was cut, like Lydia Monroe."

"She stole the makeup, special effects, and even her witch's costume from around the studio just after she was cut from the movie," Daphne points out.

58

"Which means she had been planning this for months," Fred says. "She got the job working at the concession stand so she could be close by without raising suspicion."

"It's really too bad, because now she'll never have the chance to be an actress again," Daphne adds. "When directors and producers hear about what she tried to do, they'll never hire her."

"But I'll bet you figured all this out on your own, right?" Velma asks. "I knew you could do it."

"And I hope you can come back and visit with us again soon," Daphne says. "I'm sure we'll have another exciting mystery for you to solve."

Suddenly the kitchen doors burst open and the sound of the cart with the squeaky wheel fills the restaurant.

"Hot rolls! Who wants a roll?" the man behind the cart shouts.

"Like, this time we're ready!" Shaggy announces. He and Scooby dive under the table. When they come back up, each of them is wearing a catcher's mitt and mask.

"Bring on the hot rolls!" Shaggy calls. The man behind the cart sees Shaggy and Scooby. He grabs a roll in each hand and fires them off lightning quick.

THUD! THUD! Shaggy and Scooby each catch a roll in their mitt.

"Nice catch, fellas," Daphne says. "But it's too bad you had to squish them up."

Shaggy and Scooby look down and slowly

open their mitts. With his other hand, Shaggy takes out a scrunched ball of bread, barely bigger than a Ping-Pong ball.

"Man, I hate when that happens," Shaggy complains. "What about you, Scooby?"

"Huh?" Scooby says, looking up from his

mitt. He has the slightest bit of roll left on the tip of his nose. His eyes cross as he notices it. He sticks out his big pink tongue and wipes it away.

"Rooby-rooby-roo!" he sings happily.